Dedication

This book is dedicated to the Lutheran pastors who have inspired me with their preaching, taught me, comforted me and listened patiently to my woes and ranting and raving over my lifetime. God bless you all.

Acknowledgements

Special thanks to Mary Donlon, my co-author of the Can Be Murder Series, who gave me support, encouragement and advice during the writing of this book and who was my resource on all things relating to Catholicism. Thanks also to my beta readers David Folkerds and Marcia Soule for their time and comments.

The hymn numbers referenced in the book are to Evangelical Lutheran Worship, better known as the cranberry-colored hymnal.

Foreword by Mary Donlon

When Marilyn first approached me about forming a writers' group out of a Loft Literary Center class in the suburbs of Minneapolis, I was all in. After spending twelve weeks of classes together, I knew that Marilyn was a gifted writer with a laugh-out-loud sense of humor. I looked forward to her keen eye helping me improve my own writing.

Little did I know then that some seven years later, we would be in the midst of writing our third novel together. I have been fortunate to travel this journey of being a published author with such a terrific partner, through a mystery series that sprang from her imagination. She is not only my writing partner, but a dear friend as well.

In this delightful novella, Marilyn gives us a glimpse into the life of one of the characters first introduced in our Can Be Murder Series. Told from the perspective of the Lutheran pastor of Turners Bend, it follows him one Christmas season as he questions his religious calling, while dealing with the formidable issues that come with being the head of a community church. The Pastor also struggles with his home-life balance, which includes the later-in-life pregnancy of his wife and the challenges of having adult children.

Both funny and poignant, Marilyn's characters come alive in this novella. They are utterly relatable. Whether we are from a small town like Turners Bend or from a big city, we see ourselves and our friends in the people that populate this fictional town.

What a gift.

Retrospective

Some things never change. Believe me, I've been the pastor of First Lutheran Church in Turners Bend, Iowa, for 19 years, and I know all too well. The standard joke is that Lutherans don't like change ("we've never done it that way before" being the last seven words of our faith). There's more than a bit of truth to that statement. To many folks in our congregation I'm still the new guy who may not last for long. The jury is still out.

When I look back to exactly one year ago, the day before the first Sunday in Advent, I know one person who has changed…me. I remember those four weeks with crystal-bell clarity. I weathered upheaval, discord and disillusionment and experienced majesty and miracles. Quite a combination, wouldn't you say? I'm not sure if I was being tested, but what I do know is that I witnessed the true meaning of the season with alleluias heaped upon alleluias. Amen

Chapter One

Saturday Morning

Hymn #252 "Each Winter as the Year Grows Older"

Technically, Friday and Saturday were supposed to be my two days off. But, being the solo pastor at First Lutheran, I was always on call, and there was rarely a day when I didn't spend at least some time at the church. On the Saturday before the first Sunday in Advent, I arrived at 8:00 a.m. to find several vehicles in the parking lot, some with engines running to keep the occupants warm. A few people were huddled at the door, stamping their feet. I'd come to believe that no matter what time I arrived, I would be considered late by the members of our small farming community.

I parked my twelve-year-old Honda in the "Reserved for Clergy" spot and put on my cheerful-pastor smile, readying myself to face their jives.

"You oversleep this morning, Pastor Henderson?" grumbled Hjalmer Gustafson, an eighty-year-old dairy farmer. "Time's a-wastin', young fella." He took out a blue bandana and blew his red bulbous nose that was sprouting gray hairs.

"Now, Hjalmer," said Lois his wife of fifty-five years, "I'm sure Pastor Mark has a good excuse for being tardy." Lois taught school when Turners Bend had a one-room school house for children in grades one through eight. She still sounded like a teacher and on occasion gave me a good talking to when she thought I was not properly fulfilling my role.

It was the last day of the church year. The finance committee was scheduled to do an audit of the books, the altar guild would be coming to change the paraments and set up communion for the next day and the men's fellowship group planned to erect the nativity stable out in the church yard. It was an unusually busy Saturday.

And me, I had a sermon to prepare. I had started to recycle my sermons. I would go through my file of past sermons for a particular Sunday, find one with the same gospel reading and re-work it a bit. I figured if the scripture readings could be re-used, why not the sermons? I slipped in wording such as, "You may have heard this story before, but it bears repeating." I felt guilty about it and chastised myself. I feared it was a sign of how devotion to my job was wearing thin.

I entered the office and glanced at the stack of bulletins that Sarah James, our church secretary, had printed on Friday. "Crap," I said under my breath. I had forgotten to remind her that the page numbers had to be changed back to the first setting in our hymnal, a change we made at the beginning of the church year. I would have to redo the bulletins. I made the changes on the master and placed it in our copy machine to run the copies. I no sooner started to walk down the hall to my office when the copier jammed; it was the machine Sarah always referred to as, "this hunk of junk." I returned to retrieve crumpled paper from the interior of the copier and restart the process. It was going to be a long morning.

I went to my office, sat at my desk and read over the sermon I had selected. It put forth the need to curb our excitement, not rush the season, but prepare, watch and wait for the coming of Christ. I pondered my own feelings of the moment. I had no excitement, no zeal for yet another Advent and Christmas at First Lutheran. Been here, done it, same old-same old. Frankly, I didn't give a darn anymore, which is a pretty poor attitude for a pastor. Was it a mid-career crisis, my family situation, this church, this town? I didn't know.

A small mirror was mounted on the back of my office door. I closed the door and looked at myself. Only forty-five and yet I thought I looked old. My hairline had started to recede, and I combed my hair forward to cover the bare spots. My wife Christine said I looked like a monk. I was developing jowls…when did that happen? My summer tan had faded to a pasty white. Just as I was inspecting the crow's feet at the corners of my eyes, I heard the copier clunk to a stop. Another paper jam.

"Lord have mercy."

Chapter Two

Saturday Afternoon

Hymn #249 "On Jordan's Bank the Baptist's Cry"

Some days have a dubious start, but get better; other days go right down into the sewer. Thus went the rest of my Saturday at First Lutheran...the first and only Lutheran church in Turners Bend, a town of 932 people.

I added the final touches to my sermon. I inserted that John the Baptist told the Galileans to repent and change our ways, and he wasn't just talking to the Jews. He meant Lutherans, too.

Eunice Edstrom, the chairwoman of our Altar Guild, popped into my office. She lowered her head and looked at me over the top of her glasses. "Pastor, I don't understand it. We are almost out of wine for communion and I was sure we had plenty the last time I checked."

I could see it in her face and hear it in her tone of voice. She was accusing me of sneaking nips of wine during the week. Not that I haven't been tempted at times. "No problem, Eunice, I'll stop on my way home today and pick up some more. You want the Manischewitz Concord Grape, right?"

"Very well," she said and sniffed. I never fully understood why the women of the Altar Guild sniffed at me, but knew it had something to do with disapproval. I jotted a note to myself … buy sickly-sweet cheap wine.

My next visitor was Herman Miller, head of the Finance Committee. He plopped himself down in the chair in front of my desk and said, "We got a problem, Rev."

Silence.

"You want to tell me about it, Herman?"

"Yup, I guess I better, but it's real bad."

Silence.

"Did you find a mistake in the financial records?"

"Yup."

Silence.

I wanted to yell "out with it, man," but I opted for a more pastoral remark. "I'm sure it's just some oversight that can be easily corrected. What did you find?"

"It's not what we found; it's what we didn't find."

"What didn't you find, Herman?"

"You know that endowment check from Oscar Nelson's estate?"

8

I certainly knew all about Oscar's estate. He died in a tornado a couple of years ago. He left a generous amount to First Lutheran, but it took some time before we actually received a check from his executor. The council was battling over how the money should be spent.

"Are you telling me you can't find the money in the books?"

"Nope. We can't find the money in the bank account."

My heart sunk. I had received the check and made out the deposit slip. I knew who I had given it to, but I couldn't tell Herman.

"Tell the audit committee that I'll check into it on Monday and not to worry. The money will be found and properly deposited in the account."

Herman stood, hitched up his sagging jeans, shook his head and left my office. I added Find Check to my list.

The third magi to visit my office with the gift of a problem was Frank McFadden. Frank, at the age of thirty-two, was the youngest member of the Men's Fellowship group. He always brought his grandfather, Elliott McFadden, who was wheelchair-bound, to church. Frank did the heavy lifting on projects while the rest of the group stood around giving him directions and critiquing his work. In my book, he was a saint.

I heard him chuckle and looked up to see a smile on his face. "Pastor Mark, you aren't going to believe this. You better grab your coat and come out and take a look." I put on my army surplus parka and followed him out to the yard where I found the group gathered around a pile of lumber that once was our barn-wood stable.

"What happened?" I asked.

Frank explained. "Well, Hjalmer was backing up his pick-up with the load of straw to spread in and around the stable. Says

9

he didn't hear us yell "whoa" because the earflaps were down on his hat. Whole stable when down like it was made out of toothpicks. Wood's too rotten to rebuild. Guess we'll have to start from scratch with new lumber."

"Should have looked in my rearview mirror, Pastor," said Hjalmer. He sounded a little chagrined…a rarity for the guy, who was usually full of bluster.

"I'll call the lumber yard on Monday and see if I can get Jack Murphy to deliver a load next week. Haul away the old boards and call it a day men. A new stable will be a nice change."

I could see I did not have total agreement on that last remark.

The Altar Guild women bustled out and all piled into Eunice's station wagon and drove off. They were followed by the Finance Committee. The remains of the stable were loaded in the back of trucks and carted away.

I returned to the empty church. As I passed the sanctuary, I stopped and muttered, "Lord, save me." The altar and pulpit were draped with purple paraments. Purple, not blue! The church had made the color change for Advent decades ago, and we did have a set of blue paraments hanging in the sacristy closet. Using my better judgment, I let it go.

Back in my office I added Order Lumber to my growing to-do list and placed a call to Father Bernard Kelly, my counterpart at Sacred Heart Catholic Church, the place where the other half of the town's residents worshipped.

"Bernie, Mark here. Are you finished hearing confessions?"

"No one showed up today. Seems there are no sinners in my parish anymore."

"You up for hearing mine over at the Bend?"

"Any place is holy where two or more are gathered. I'll be there before you can say your Hail Mary and Our Father."

Chapter Three

Hymn #255 "There's a Voice in the Wilderness"

The Bend was Turners Bend's only drinking establishment. Established in 1962, it had undergone only two changes since that date. About ten years ago Joe Garcia, the owner and bartender, added a retail bottle shop when the town's liquor store relocated out on the highway next to the then-new Walmart. Last year he installed a fifty-two inch HD television and announced that the place was now a sports bar.

When I entered the dimly lit room, it was empty. Brenda Lee's "I'm Sorry" was playing on the jukebox, and Joe was singing along in a pretty fine baritone voice. He knew the words to all the Golden Oldies in his jukebox collection. He stopped mid-tune and greeted me.

"Howdy, Pastor Mark. Take a stool, any stool."

"I've never seen this place empty before, Joe. What's up?"

"Hawkeyes have a bye this week and there's an invitational basketball tournament over at the high school." High school basketball was big in Turners Bend, and the Prairie Dogs had a loyal following.

Joe checked the big clock behind the bar. "My regulars should be showing up about five or so. What can I get for you?"

"First, do you have any of our communion wine in stock?"

"Sure do. I order it just for First Lutheran. No one else would buy that crappy stuff. His Eminence prefers a good Spanish red."

"Put two bottles on my tab and remind me to take it when I leave. And speaking of Bernie, he'll be here shortly. Set up two boilermakers for us."

"Whoa, that bad, huh? Coming right up?" He turned as we heard the door opening. "Here's the good father right now."

Father Kelly was short and round. His once red hair had turned white, but the twinkle in his eyes belied a man much livelier than one would expect in a seventy-nine-year-old man. Unlike me, he usually wore his clerical collar in public and today was no exception. After a pilgrimage to Ireland he perfected an Irish accent, which usually appeared after a beer or two. I genuinely liked the man and we were confidants and good friends. He slapped me on the back and gave Joe a high-five as the bartender put two glasses of amber brew in front of us.

Joe moved to the end of the long mahogany bar and displayed the skill that had made him famous in Boone county. He slid the first glass of whiskey down the bar and it stopped directly in front of Bernie. Then he did the same with my glass of whiskey. He called it Bartender Bocce.

14

Bernie and I picked up our drinks and moved to a table to be out of Joe's hearing and away from the jukebox, now playing "Blue Velvet."

Bernie gave his usual toast. "This is the day that the Lord has made, let us rejoice and be glad in it." We clinked glasses and sipped the foam off the top of our beers.

"So it's a confession you'll be wantin' to make," he said. "Spill the beans, boy."

I hesitated. Where to start? "To say that I am weary of it all sounds lame, but that's about it in a nutshell."

Bernie took a sip of his whiskey and waited for me to continue.

"Here it is the beginning of a new church year, the start of Advent, and Christmas right around the corner, and I'm more than a pint low on energy for the whole ordeal. I'm beginning to wonder if I'm fit to be a pastor anymore. We've got a busted stable, missing communion wine, a lost endowment check and purple paraments, and frankly to quote Rhett Butler, 'I don't give a damn'."

"Hardly seems like the stuff to cause a crisis of faith. What's lost will be found and what's busted will be repaired, and purple is a lovely color for Advent. I suspect there's more to it than that," he said. "So how is the blossoming Christine?"

The man could read me like a book. He hit it right in the middle of the dart board. Christine, my wife. Christine, my *pregnant* wife.

"I don't know, Bernie. Marta and Leif are almost adults. We were going to down-size, go back to Minneapolis to be near our aging parents, look for a call in a city church, move on to the next stage of our lives, but now..." I halted, realizing I sounded like a spoiled child.

"And what about Christine? How does she feel about this glitch in your plans?"

"That's what's so hard. Christine is thrilled. She's acting like a first-time mother, calling him our 'caboose child.' She's brushing off all the doctor's warnings and precautions about change-of-life babies. She's refusing to see how embarrassed our older children probably are."

"In other words, she's accepting this babe as a gift from God."

Ah, leave it to my priest friend. He would have to bring God into it and set me straight. How many times have I preached that gifts from God...grace, unconditional love, all creatures great and small...are freely given to us?

The changer on the jukebox shifted and the Shirelles reminded me in song "Mama said there would be days like this."

Chapter Four

First Sunday in Advent

Hymn #259 "Fling Wide the Door"

My Sunday morning routine never varies. I arrive one hour before the ushers and go through a mental check list. I'm afraid to deviate from it for fear of forgetting something crucial. I've had nightmares of stepping to the pulpit and not finding my sermon notes or forgetting to turn on the coffeemaker and causing a mass riot in the fellowship hall after the service.

I opened the door to the youth room and turned on the light. It looked different to me, too neat, almost like someone had organized the clutter and dusted. The usual garbage was actually in the trash can. I'd have to check with our custodian.

Up to now he had refused to clean up after our teenagers, declaring their room a toxic zone. Maybe he had a change of heart or just couldn't stand the mess anymore.

I began to robe in my office. I reached for my alb and realized it was blue. I searched for my purple one and couldn't find it. I would have to do with the multi-colored one that the quilting group had gifted me last year. I would be in deep doo-doo with the ladies of the Altar Guild, but that was nothing new.

The ushers arrived, put on their name tags, grabbed stacks of bulletins and manned their posts by the sanctuary doors. They didn't have to seat people because everyone always sat in the same spot. I could look out and instantly know who was missing. It was my practice to check up on those people on Monday, which seems to keep our attendance strong. I can imagine someone like Hjalmer saying he didn't feel like going to church, and Lois saying in her school marm-voice, "You know Pastor Henderson will call you tomorrow, and you'll have to have a good excuse. Feeling like not going will not suffice, dear heart."

I stood in the narthex to greet members by name. I knew my flock. Eunice arrived, lifted her eyebrows and sniffed when she saw my alb. At least I remembered the wine, which might atone for some of my transgressions.

Christine arrived. With her due date being just six weeks away, she was looking very pregnant, much bigger than I remember with our first two children. Marta was almost twenty and a student at Luther College. She would be home at the end of the semester. Our son, Leif, was working at a gas station in Boone. He always seemed to be scheduled to work on Sunday morning, a sore point with me.

Christine's winter coat could no longer be buttoned, and it hung open to reveal her belly. She smiled and gave me a little wave. My heart fluttered. I had to admit she did look radiant and happy. There had never been any doubt in her mind about going through with this pregnancy. I was the doubter, the worrier. I struggled with this decision but my conversation with Bernie had begun to turn me around, or as John the Baptist would say to repent, as in the Greek-meaning of the word.

Christine and I met at Gustavus Adolphus College in St. Peter, Minnesota, when she was a freshman and I was a senior, a BMOC ever since I had announced my intention of attending Luther Seminary and becoming an ordained Lutheran pastor. She was not impressed, turned up her cute little nose at me and told me politely that she was not interested in dating me. It was game-on and I eventually convinced her otherwise. She claims to this day that she was merely employing reverse psychology on me.

In the narthex Christine was immediately surrounded by women, busy bees buzzing around a lovely flower. Her church friends have pitched in and relieved her of all the pastor's wife's duties she had so willingly dispensed over the years. She was rather enjoying her break from directing the children's choir, leading the women's bible study group, making lefse for the upcoming bake sale and a host of other tasks. The previous night she told me, "Being over forty and seven and a half months pregnant is the best excuse ever for doing nothing and being waited on hand and foot. I'm loving this."

The service had a few missteps, nothing catastrophic, but enough to give me a slight feeling of unease. The organist forgot to give me my cue note for the liturgy and I started out too high, the wick on the first Advent candle was pesky and wouldn't light, singing all the verses of every hymn made us run over by five minutes, and I saw a lot of watch-checking during communion.

I also saw something else from my vantage point of being the only one facing the congregation. I saw a newcomer, a young black-haired woman with an infant in her arms. She came in after the entrance hymn and departed before communion. She looked vaguely familiar but I couldn't place her.

Coffee hour after the service was more important to some of our members than the worship service itself. Bernice Larson, owner of Bernice's Main Street Bakery, arrived every Sunday with freshly baked rolls and cookies. That morning she set aside a maple-frosted Long John for me, knowing I would be the last to join the assembled crowd in the fellowship hall. A long-time waitress at the Cinnamon Bun Café, she won a national baking contest and started her own bakery in town last year. She confessed to me that she also baked an equal amount for Sacred Heart. She referred to it as being ecumenical, and I told her God meant for all dominations to have her heavenly food. She liked that and thought she might be able to work it into her next marketing slogan.

Just as in church, people tended to sit at the same tables with the same people every Sunday. I stopped by the men's table to see what had the guys so eagerly watching Lance Williams. Lance was once a Chicago architect and now owned an organic farm in Turners Bend. He was sketching a diagram on the back of the service bulletin. I stood over his shoulder to observe and listen in on the conversation.

"I'm thinking bi-level with a croft for hay and maybe a built-in manger over here and animal stalls here. We could use that new pressure-treated wood, and stain it with an oil-based stain," he said as he drew his plan. "Then for the roof, I suggest pre-rusted steel."

I walked away. I could see we would end up with the Cadillac of nativity stables, one that would likely put a big dent in our properties budget.

Chapter Five

First Week of Advent

Hymn #241 "O Lord, How Shall I Meet You"

I sat at my desk and looked at the to-do list I had written on Saturday and crossed off the wine. Was there really wine missing? I couldn't be sure, but that was the least of my worries. Next on my list was Find Check. Dread covered me like a cold, wet wool blanket. Should I question Sarah James or just call the bank and Oscar's lawyer to try to stop payment and get a new check issued? I imagined it would not be easy to get another check for $15,000…at least not quickly and not without a lot of paperwork. Maybe Sarah knew where the check was, although I had grave doubts.

First Lutheran had the same secretary for thirty-two years. Mildred Skogmo was a paragon of efficiency. The answer to any question around the church was always, "Ask Mildred." The woman saved my butt more times than I care to mention.

She retired and sadly died six months later, taking all of the congregation's vital information to the grave with her. She was replaced by Sarah James.

Since then the phrase most often heard around the church was, "poor Sarah." Sarah was a farmer's daughter, married to a farmer, or should I say, former farmer. Her husband, James (yes, James James), lost the family farm, a loss all too frequently experienced by many family farmers in our county. The land and equipment were auctioned off and the family of seven, with five children under ten, moved into town. The only work James could find was at Walmart. It was clear that Sarah would have to find a job. The Personnel Committee hired her, not for her skills, but because she desperately needed work.

Sarah's computer skills were minimal. Her organizational and time management skills weak, and her memory elusive. I thought at first she might improve with time as she learned the job, but that was a pipe dream. To give her due credit, she was great at talking with people who dropped by the church office or called on the phone. She was an ace chit-chatter and was able to keep me up to date on the scuttlebutt traveling through the congregation.

I was kicking myself for giving her the check to deposit into our account at the Community Bank of Turners Bend, although she did make the weekly deposits of offering every Monday. I remembered I was late for one of Christine's ultra-sound appointments that day, and I wanted to get the check deposited as soon as possible.

I checked my watch. Sarah was just arriving, twenty-five minutes late.

"Morning, Pastor," she yelled in her hog-calling voice.

I walked to the front office and sat in the chair next to her desk. "Morning Sarah. How are the kids?"

"Pokey and whiney, just like they are every Monday morning. Junior left his lunch in the car and I had to turn around and go back to school. Megan lost her first tooth and took it to Show and Tell, and the baby is cutting his first tooth. We got teeth coming and going at our house." She laughed.

I took a deep breath and dove into the murky waters of her memory. "Sarah, remember that check I gave you to deposit last week, the one from Oscar Nelson's estate?"

"Sure, it was a whopper of a check, right?"

"Yes. And did you deposit the check?"

"Why, yes, I'm sure I must have."

"You're sure? You took it to Community Bank?"

"Well, I sort of remember putting it on the counter, so I would see it when I left. Now let me see. Was that the day the school nurse called me to come and get Jenny when she threw up on her teacher's desk?"

"Do you think that check could still be around here someplace? It hasn't shown up in our account." I was doing pretty good at not sounding totally exasperated, which I was, of course.

"It could be, because I was in kind of a rush that day."

"Do you think you could search for it and see if it just happens to still be here?"

Her face scrunched up and tears began to leak out of the corners of her eyes. I could see she was working up to a big sob-fest, not the first I had witnessed. Sarah was a first-class crier.

"Oh Pastor, I don't think I took it to the bank. This is all my fault. What am I going to do? We don't have any money to repay the church. The kids have all outgrown their clothes, and

23

James needs a root canal, and I'm overwhelmed. It was James who wanted a big farm family and now we don't even have a farm and four of the kids are sleeping in the same bed." The flood gates were open and she grabbed a wad of tissues from the box on her desk.

I let her cry it out and ramble off her long list of woes. When she stopped to take a breath, I patted her shoulder and said, "I'll help you find it, Sarah. I'm sure it's here in the office somewhere. Go make us a pot of coffee in the kitchen, and I'll start a search. Remember the Lord will provide. He will not give us more than we can handle."

I made mental notes to call our local social service agency to see if they could give the James family some assistance, especially with clothing and toys for the kids for Christmas, and to add some bonus money from my discretionary fund to her next pay check.

I first searched her desktop and desk drawers. I moved on to the recycling bin and was examining each piece of paper one-by-one when Sarah returned with two mugs of coffee and two chocolate donuts left over from Sunday.

"Nothing yet, why don't you go through your handbag?"

Sarah finished off a donut and then dumped her over-sized bag onto the top of her desk. She found one child's sock, an unpaid parking ticket from a trip to Ames, a pacifier covered with lint, a week-old sandwich squished in a sandwich baggie, but no check.

I ate my donut, fortifying myself before suggesting I search her car. "You watch the phone, Sarah, and I'll have a look in your car. Just give me the keys."

Easier said, than done. It took her five minutes to locate her car keys, which had fallen through a hole in her jacket pocket and into the lining. I prepared myself for the interior of her old Dodge station wagon, and it did not disappoint. I dug through smelly soccer jerseys, school papers, candy bar wrappers, empty baby bottles and overdue library books. I was just about to give up when I opened a greasy fast food bag and found the check. "Praise the Lord for blessings great and small."

I trotted back to the office and waved the check triumphantly in Sarah's face. She was chit-chatting on the phone, but gave me a high-five and a huge grin.

I crossed the check off my list and moved on to Order Lumber. I had become adept at the art of delegation. I did not want to become directly involved in the construction of the new stable, so I placed a call to Lance Williams.

"Lance, Pastor Mark here. I'd appreciate it if you would head up the stable project. Just give Jack Murphy at the lumber yard a call, order what you need and tell him we'd appreciate a discount. Oh, and remind him to use our tax exempt number. I know I can trust you to do a bang-up job. First Lutheran is darn lucky to have someone with your expertise."

It worked like a charm; a little flattery, coupled with no opportunity to really decline, and I was able to cross that item off my list. It was almost noon and I was yet to start my hospital and shut-in visits and absent member calls.

I had meant to ask Sarah about the woman and baby I had seen in the back pew as I left, but when I passed her desk she was still yakking on the phone.

Chapter Six

Second Week of Advent

Hymn #257 "O Come, O Come, Emmanuel"

The second Sunday in Advent was bitter cold. A heavy gray sky foretold of snow to come, and parishioners bent into a biting wind from the northwest as they ventured from their cars. It did not stop them, however, from taking a tour of the stable which had been finished on Saturday. During the week enough building supplies to erect a barn had been delivered, and the construction crew labored from first light to dusk to build the Taj Mahal of stables.

I watched out my office window as Lance Williams, dressed as a shepherd, pointed out the features of our new stable. The man had a flair for drama, and he and his wife Lucinda, a New York literary agent, brought a touch of Hollywood razzle-dazzle to our staid little town.

Hanging with my robe was a new purple alb, compliments of the quilting group. I expected a nod of approval from Eunice and her cohorts. As I dressed, I began to brace myself for the anthem of the day. Isabelle Johnson, the church's oldest soprano would be warbling her way through "O Come, O Come, Emmanuel." I had a tough time dissuading her from singing all eight verses. We compromised on five. God bless her; the woman had staying power.

Christine's feet had begun to swell and she was staying home. I knew I would get lots of questions about her welfare. People took note when she was not sitting in the front pew. I was seeing signs that this pregnancy was taking its toll on her, but she insisted she was just fine. I was thankful that she was seeing Doc Schultz every week from now until she delivered.

The service and fellowship hour went without incident. As I was hanging up my robe and preparing to leave for the day, the nursery coordinator stuck her head in my office.

"Sorry to bother you, Pastor Mark, but we need disposable diapers in the nursery. We had two full boxes last week and I used the last one on Peter James this morning. I had to send the McFadden baby home with a diaper that badly needed changing. Where in the world did all those diapers go?"

"Are you sure the custodian didn't put them out of the way? In a cupboard or storeroom some place."

"I asked him and he said no."

I dipped into our petty cash fund and gave her money to buy more diapers. Then I added missing diapers to my mental list of strange happenings around First Lutheran.

Before I left, I looked at the calendar for the week. I would need to put my feet up alongside of Christine's to rest for the mayhem ahead.

***

I was ten minutes behind schedule, and they were waiting for me Monday morning...the bakers. All week a group of women and a few retired men would be invading the kitchen to prepare for Saturday's holiday bake sale and craft boutique. The schedule had remained the same for decades: Monday lefse, Tuesday spritz, Wednesday, krumkake, Thursday rosettes and Friday packaging and pricing. They would break for coffee and treats at 10 a.m. and I was expected to join them. Then they would finish at noon, eat lunch and clean up for the day.

"We were worried when you were so late, Pastor. Is Christine okay?" asked Eunice. I wanted to say ten minutes was not really that late, but I refrained. Eunice was becoming my cross to bear.

"She's fine. Just a little tired." In truth, Christine had had a fitful night, and her discomfort kept both of us up. This group was prone to over-reacting, and I didn't want them disturbing Christine with calls and visits.

Hjalmer, who had been inspecting the stable, joined the group. "Some of us were just commenting that Mr. Williams went overboard on that new stable. We could have saved a lot of money by building something more modest, don't you think?"

There was no way I was going to weigh in on that conversation. I wanted to remind Hjalmer that he was the one who rammed into the old stable, but again I bit my tongue. No matter what we spent money on at First, there was always some penny-pincher who complained about the expense.

The bakers unloaded their cars and trooped into the kitchen, and I went to my office, hoping to get some work done before my coffee break appearance. The phone was ringing as I entered the office. I grabbed it.

"First Lutheran. This is Pastor Henderson speaking." It was Sarah saying that Junior and Jenny had the stomach flu and were going from both ends (her words) and that she wouldn't be able to make it into work.

"No problem, Sarah. I can manage okay. Hope the kids are well enough for the children's Christmas program. Don't forget there is a dress rehearsal on Wednesday night."

Christine had directed the Christmas program ever since we were called to First. This year Lucinda Williams had taken over, and the program had turned into an extravaganza of Broadway proportions. New costumes, new scenery and props, klieg lights with colored gels, and a script written by our local crime writer, Chip Collingsworth. It was either a delight or a disaster in the making; I wasn't sure which one. I was trying to stay out of it, although I felt obliged to remind Lucinda that the script in the second chapter of Luke was hard to improve upon.

I settled into my office chair and read over the gospel for the third Sunday in Advent. Again, I hunted up an old sermon and was reading it when Father Kelly showed up.

I greeted him and offered him a chair. "You old rascal. I know why you're here this morning," I said. "In a word, it's lefse."

"I cannot tell a lie. My name may be Kelly but my mother was an Anderson, and I could smell that lefse baking all the way over at Sacred Heart. Plus I never forget the baking schedule over here. I can still hear my sainted mother giving me instructions on the proper rolling out of the dough. I have the lefse stick she used to flip them on the grill. I use it as a back scratcher. I was hoping your bakers might give this old priest a taste of his boyhood."

"You're so full of blarney. You know those women adore you. I think they like you better than they do me. They'll be expecting you as usual, Bernie."

He laughed and his merriment lightened my mood.

"Say, I took a look at that new stable. Quite the edifice. I was down at the Cinnamon Bun Café early this morning and Doctor Jane, our wonderful red-haired vet, was talking about bringing in live animals on Christmas Eve. Not just a donkey, but sheep and a cow and goats and pigs, too."

"News to me, but sometimes I swear I'm the last to know what's going on around here. I'm feeling like this whole season has gotten out of control. I just can't get into the mood, the right frame of mind."

Bernie leaned back in the chair, crossed his legs and templed his fingers together. "You haven't talked about him recently, Mark. Is it the boy?"

Leif, my son. Bernie always refers to him as "the boy."

"He comes and goes from the house, but we go for days without seeing him, much less talking with him. He's working hard at the Kum & Go, but it upsets me that he's not in school. He should be off to college like his friends. He does seem to be staying clean and sober, and going to AA and seeing his parole officer. I suppose I should be grateful for that."

"You suppose?" Bernie said as he raised his bushy white eyebrows.

"Ah, Bernie, you have a way of slapping me upside the head, don't you? I am grateful. He could be in jail, he could be jobless and homeless and shooting up in some dive. He could be dead from drugs and booze. I need an attitude adjustment, don't I?"

"I pray for him every day, you know. I'll pray for you, too, my friend. Now let's adjourn to the kitchen and see if those lovely women could put a little butter and sugar on some lefse for us old sinners."

Chapter Seven

Third Week of Advent

Hymn# 286 "Your Little Ones, Dear Lord"

The bake sale on Saturday had gone well. Doc Shultz had put Christine on bed rest, so there wouldn't be any baking in our house until Marta came home from Luther College at the end of the week. I brought home lefse for Christine and fudge for myself.

Marta, our oldest, was a typical first child, an over-achiever, a conference all-star basketball player, a talented organist and academic scholarship winner, who was in her senior year. After graduation she planned to go to grad school to study bio-ethics and hospital administration. No wonder Leif went the other direction. It was hard to compete with her.

Leif started to skip school in the tenth grade and went down a slippery slope from there until the past year. Petty crime, booze, drugs, he ended up in treatment and on probation. He did not graduate with his class, but since passed his GED. He caused Christine and me many sleepless nights and much soul-searching. Where did we gone wrong?

There's a lot of pressure on preacher's kids. PK's or TO's (theological offspring) are put up to higher standards than other kids, especially in small towns. Marta accepted the challenge and Leif rebelled against it. It worried me that we were now going to put another child to the test.

Before I went through my Sunday morning routine I sent Marta a text message to confirm she had a ride home from Decorah after she finished her finals. If all went according to schedule, she would be with us when our new son was born in mid-January.

The day of the much-anticipated children's program had arrived. The performance was scheduled for three in the afternoon. I took a look at the programs that had arrived from the printer. The front had a water-color rendition of our new stable, nestled in snow on a starry night. I opened it to the title page: **Who is this mysterious child?** Nice, I liked it. Lucinda Williams had shooed me away from rehearsals, saying she wanted the program to be a surprise for me. I didn't have the heart (or guts) to tell her that I am not especially fond of surprises. I was feeling sad that Christine would miss it, but the doctor had been quite adamant about her staying off her feet and had ordered bed rest for the duration of her pregnancy.

I robed and went into the narthex to greet the arriving worshipers. There seemed to be an unusual amount of buzzing about the upcoming program. I saw a group of women clustered together. Eunice was in the center writing a list. I moved closer to eavesdrop.

"I'll bring a meatloaf dinner tomorrow night and Alice will bring beef stew on Tuesday. How about you Betty, can you handle Wednesday night?"

They had to be planning meals for us. We hadn't told anyone about Christine's bed rest. How did they know? Sometimes I was amazed at how fast and far news traveled in Turners Bend.

After the morning service and coffee hour, I went home to fix some lunch for Christine and myself. I arrived to find Bernice in our kitchen.

"Oh hi, Pastor. Sit yourself down and take a load off. Lunch will be ready in about ten minutes. I hope you like Tater Tot Hot dish and Waldorf salad. The crescent rolls are just coming out of the oven and the pineapple upside down cake is cooling. I thought I'd dish everything up and you and Christine can eat on TV trays in the living room." She never stopped moving while she was talking, pans and dishes were flying left and right.

"Bless you, Bernice."

"Gosh, it's not much. I just threw some stuff together. Your dinner is in the fridge. You'll just have to heat it in the microwave when you come home from the Christmas program. I hear it's going to be something else. Lucinda has outdone herself. Junior James has the starring role of the detective."

I stopped dead in my tracks. "Detective?"

"Sure, Chip wrote the script. It's a mystery, you know."

Chapter Eight

Children's Christmas Program

Hymn# 296 "What Child Is This"

After Bernice's feast, Christine took a nap. I took a cell phone picture of her dressed in my ratty old terrycloth robe, the one she had monogrammed and gave to me for our first Christmas together, and a pair of bright pink slipper socks. Then I kissed her gently on the head and drove back to church for the afternoon program.

The parking lot was already full of vehicles, including a van from the local cable TV company, a truck from a rental company in Ames and a pickup with an attached horse trailer. Hjalmer had donned a reflective vest and was directing traffic. I parked in my reserved spot and sat in my car for a few minutes working up enough courage to face the hoopla within.

I expected to be surprised, but the scene in the narthex was a stunner. The tall, good-looking Lance Williams, dressed in a tuxedo, a microphone in hand, was interviewing people on a red carpet runner. The cable TV cameras were rolling as he posed questions to his wife Lucinda, who was decked out in a shimmery red dress and a load of bling.

"You are the creative genius behind this production, Lucinda. What was your conceptual image for the program?" asked Lance.

"Shock and awe," said Lucinda. "I wanted a performance that would blow the audience away and send them home inspired by the rediscovery of Jesus' birth."

"Good luck tonight. I know you will more than deliver on your dream."

Lucinda hurried away and Father Kelly replaced her on the red carpet.

"Father Kelly, may I be so bold as to ask what prompted the attendance of a Roman Catholic priest at this event?"

"Well, Mr. Williams. The story is universal and I never get tired of hearing it. Plus, I've been hearing of nothing else for the past few weeks. I think you'll find more than a few of us from Sacred Heart here today." As Bernie walked off, he spied me and gave a thumbs-up sign.

Next up were our town veterinarian, Jane Swanson, and her crime writer husband, Chip Collingsworth. It pleased me no end to see them together and happily married. Jane was a native of Turners Bend, but Chip came to town from Baltimore a few years ago. His arrival was followed by that of his literary agent, Lucinda Williams, nee Patterson, and Lance. The three of them transformed our decaying town into a hub of excitement, and it looked like tonight would be no different.

Lance launched into his interview with Chip. "Mr. Collingsworth wrote the script for tonight. You're a crime writer of national fame. What inspired you to take on a children's play for a church?"

The bespectacled writer chuckled. "As you know, it is difficult to say no to my literary agent. Let's just say that Lucinda was very persuasive."

"And Dr. Swanson," said Lance, as he turned his attention to Jane, "I hear there will be animals in the production, is that right?"

"Oh yes. Even our three-legged dog Runt has a speaking part."

As I listened to the interviews I was both intrigued and horrified. My imagination began to run wild. A dog, shock and awe, a script written by a crime writer, a detective. It was all too much for me. I wanted to sneak into the sanctuary and find a seat in the last pew, but I couldn't escape Lance.

"We have time for one last interview and here is the pastor of First Lutheran, the Reverend Mark Henderson. Would you like to say a few words to our cable channel viewers?"

I was trapped. I stepped onto the red carpet and mumbled a few words of thanks and ended with "enjoy the performance." Oh Lord, I sounded more like a movie producer than the spiritual leader of this church. I said a silent prayer that the bishop would not see this.

What followed was indescribably miraculous. Funny, moving, visually beautiful, inspiring...I couldn't come up with enough adjectives. The plot was a mystery, but all the key elements of the traditional Christmas story were cleverly incorporated into the script.

Junior removed his cloak to reveal his true identity. "I am really a detective for the Bethlehem Police Department," he boomed. "I was working undercover as an innkeeper. Something mysterious is happening here tonight and rumors are flying about the birth of a special baby. Do not fear, folks, I'll solve this case and find out who this child is."

Singing in sweet little voices the procession of characters moved down the aisle, shepherds trailed by baby lambs, angels holding sparkling wands, the three magi and the holy family.

Our old ragged costumes, previously made of bathrobes, sheets, drapes and shawls, had been replaced by elaborate costumes of satins and brocades. The angels' tinsel halos were gone. Their halos were glowing phosphorescent tubes and each angel wore tiny feather wings. The shepherds' staffs, which until now had been broomsticks and canes, were tall, gnarled pieces of polished wood. The coats of the magi were so long that each had a servant to carry them as they processed down the aisle bearing gifts that looked like they came from Tiffany's.

Jenny James, Sarah's oldest daughter, was Mary. She road in on a live donkey (or was it a mule?), and the spotlight remained on her throughout the performance, giving her an ethereal appearance. Her baby brother, playing Jesus, remained peacefully in the manger and didn't cry.

During his investigation Junior first questioned the shepherds. "Can you describe the angel that visited you in the fields while you were tending your flock?"

"Yes, sir, it was an angel of the Lord and glory shone all around and then there was a host of angels singing," said one of the shepherds, whereupon a trio of little angels sang "Angels We Have Heard on High."

"Very curious." Junior jotted his findings in a little notebook and turned to the three wise men. "You are strangers in these parts. What brings you to Bethlehem?"

The wise men answered in song with "We Three Kings."

"I'll have to see your passports and visas, and I see you have a dog. Does that dog have a proper license?"

Runt, Chip's three-legged dog, barked on cue; the audience laughed and a few children tittered.

"Do you know who this baby is?" asked one of the wise men.

Junior answered. "I can't comment because this is an ongoing police investigation. I will have a press conference as soon as I interrogate Mary and Joseph, the parents of this baby.

"Alright, step back everyone. I'm going into the stable and check out the manger where this baby lies." Junior moved into the stable, while the children sang "Away in the Manger."

He returned from the stable, donned a Sherlock Holmes-like deerstalker hat and held up a spyglass. He waited like a professional comedian for the laughter, and then addressed the crowd, "The mystery has been solved. The child born today is the long awaited Messiah, our Lord and Savior Jesus Christ."

It was the ending though that was the show-stopper. The lights were dimmed and all the children stood along the outer aisles holding battery-powered candles. Star-like lights appeared all across the vaulted ceiling of the nave and a few traveled like comets. Then seemingly out of nowhere, dressed as an angel, little Joshua McFadden rose into the air. Hovering about us he sang "Oh Holy Night" in his pitch-perfect boy soprano voice to the hushed audience. Then he appeared to fade away in a cloud.

The lights went up and the crowd stood and clapped and hooted, many wiping away tears.

Chapter Nine

Last Week of Advent

Hymn#258 "Unexpected and Mysterious"

The Christmas program had lifted my spirits and put me in a much more festive frame of mind. It helped that my daughter Marta was home. Her ride had dropped her off at the church in time to catch the program. When she and I arrived home, she took one look at the still-to-be-decorated tree, the unwrapped gifts, and the pile of laundry that I had promised Christine I would do, and she dug right in to the tasks.

When I left the house on Monday morning mother and daughter were discussing the menus for Christmas Eve and Christmas Day. I had been worrying about leaving Christine alone, but Marta's presence eased my anxiousness.

I unlocked the front door to the church and my happiness balloon burst. The narthex was full of costumes and equipment and trash. But, taped to the door of my office was a note from Lucinda. It read: *Pastor Mark, Do not fear for I bring you great news (ha ha). A cleaning crew is scheduled to arrive at 10 a.m. and the rental company will pick up the equipment at noon. Lucinda Williams.*

Sarah arrived still on cloud nine over her children's performances. When she wasn't chit-chatting with the cleaning crew and rental company driver, she was talking on the phone. She did handle the calls from two local newspapers that wanted to do stories on the program, but otherwise, I got little work out of her.

"Pastor Mark, I need forgiveness for ever saying I didn't want five children. My children are remarkable. Why Junior just knocked my socks off. I think he has an acting career in his future. And my Jenny, wasn't she a beautiful Mary?"

"They surely are a blessing. Even the baby was perfect."

"Well, I have to confess that a good dose of children's cough syrup did make him drowsy."

I was just about to remind her of the three service bulletins we had to prepare when the phone rang, and she was occupied for the next hour.

I went to my office, shut the door and dug through my old files. I needed to come up with something clever for the Christmas Eve children's sermon. All my old sermons were dated. I had lost touch with the latest fads and animated characters. What had replaced Pokemon and Strawberry Shortcake? I hadn't the vaguest idea. It struck me that Christine and I would be returning to the world of babies and toddlers soon. The thought made me feel old and tired.

On Tuesday Marta offered to help with the bulletins. In three hours she accomplished what would have taken Sarah all week to do. The bulletins were written, copied and bundled by noon.

She sat in the chair in front of my desk with a serious look on her face. "Dad, Leif needs to tell you something. He's coming here on his lunch hour."

I felt confused and more than a little blind-sided. "Leif? You've talked with Leif? I didn't think you had much contact with him."

"We text all the time and talk by phone at least once a week. He is my brother, you know. He's pretty nervous about talking with you, so he wanted me to intercede and be here to have his back."

"I don't understand. Is this something that we should do at home and include your mother?"

"Mother already knows." Marta shook her head. "Dad, you never seem to get it. Mom always knows what's happening with us, even when we don't tell her directly. It must be a mother thing. She's been encouraging Leif to tell you himself."

As we waited for Leif to arrive, I prepared myself for bad news. In my career I had listened to a lot of bad news and counseled parishioners through times of heartache and loss and tragedies and troubles of all kinds. It's a whole different story, however, when it's my own family, and I felt ill with dread.

As he entered my office, I was dismayed that I seemingly had missed his transition from teenage boy to man. He was no longer skinny and gangly. He had filled out and sported that unshaven look that seemed to be the fashion among movie stars. He wore his Kum & Go uniform with his name embroidered on the jacket pocket.

Marta gave him a hug and kiss. "Go ahead, Leif," she encouraged him.

"I've got to get back to work and I want to get this over, so here goes." He took a deep breath, cleared his throat, then halted.

I was dumbfounded and murmured, "Okay, shoot."

"Do you remember Melissa Carter from high school?"

"Vaguely. Didn't she drop out of school and move away during your junior year? Petite brunette?"

"Yes, but she has black hair now, and she's back in town with her baby girl, Ava. I met up with her again at AA, and I've sort of been helping her. Her parents won't have anything to do with her, and she has nowhere to live. I've been saving up for an apartment and finally was able to rent one in Boone for us."

"And your mother knows about this?"

"Yes, she's the one who gave me the church key."

I felt like I was under water. Everything he was saying was garbled and swirling around in my head. Black-haired girl with a baby, church key, apartment. I couldn't sort it all out. A thought about the baby drifted into my consciousness.

"Leif, are you telling me Ava is your child?"

"Oh my God no, Dad. Ava's father is out of the picture, at least for 18-20 years. He's in prison for dealing drugs. I'm moving in with them because I want to take care of them. And well, I sort of like her a lot, a whole lot. We kind of love each other and we both love Ava bunches."

I took a moment to digest this and then remembered the church key. "What does the church key have to do with this?"

Leif's leg began to bounce, just like it did when he was nervous as a kid. "For a while Melissa and Ava were staying in the church at night, sleeping in the youth room. I'd let them in late at night and pick them up early in the morning."

Things started to click for me. "The missing diapers?"

"Yes, we used some of the diapers from the nursery and some of the food from the kitchen, but I put money in the offering box for that stuff."

"And the missing wine?"

"I don't know anything about missing wine. Believe me Dad, Melissa and I are clean and sober, and we're going to stay that way." He looked at his watch. "I've got to go, but I wanted to know if I could bring them to the house for Christmas. Would you be okay with that, Dad?"

"This is a lot for me to absorb, Leif. But of course, people who are important to you are always welcome in our home. I'm proud of you. Your mother and I never doubted that you have a heart full of kindness. You're taking on a lot of responsibility but making good decisions. We'll support you in any way we can."

The look of relief on my son's face was priceless, and the tears streaming down Marta's face were a sign to me that everything was going to be okay with the Henderson family.

Chapter Ten

Five Days Before Christmas

Hymn # 254 "Come, Thou Long-Expected Jesus"

Christine and I talked far into the night. We talked about the hopes and fears for our children, born and unborn. We pondered the benefits and downsides of being parents again at our age and so many years after the birth of our last child. As dawn neared we narrowed down the list of names for our new son, a favorite topic of Christine's. She favored Swedish family names and I was pushing for a biblical name.

"What about Oskar, spelled with a k?" she suggested.

"Are you kidding me? The kid would be teased with the Oscar Mayer wiener song his whole life. What's wrong with one of the four gospels?"

"Nothing dear, but they're so ordinary, what about Kristoff with a K?"

"What about Christopher spelled the normal way?"

And so our discussion continued until well after midnight. No agreement and no decision made.

Early Wednesday morning, as I was nursing my first cup of coffee, I gave Sarah a call. "Take the rest of the week off, Sarah. It'll be my Christmas gift to you. Stay home and enjoy those rising movie stars of yours."

Needless to say, I made Sarah's day. It was also a gift of sorts to myself. I looked forward to having three days of peace and quiet to relax and prepare spiritually for First Lutheran's coming worship services.

On the way to church the first snowflakes of December began to dance in the air. Ah, a white Christmas after all, every Midwesterner's dream, I thought to myself.

I completed my morning routine in the church. Passing the sacristy, I remembered the missing wine. The mysteries of the clean youth room, lost check and missing diapers had been solved. But what about the wine? The two bottles I purchased were on the counter. I rummaged through the robe closet and found a paper bag with two unopened bottles of wine. Someone on the Altar Guild stashed them away and forgot about them. Memory loss was catching up with Eunice and a few of her cohorts. I said, "Eureka, another mystery solved," when someone tapped me on the shoulder making me scream like a teenage girl.

"Little early in the morning to be sneaking the communion grape, isn't it, my friend?" Father Bernie was standing with two tall coffees and a bag from Bernice's Main Street Bakery, an elfish smile on his face.

"Bernie, you old goat, you scared the crap out of me. I see you are bearing gifts that are even better than frankincense and myrrh."

We settled in my office and savored the lattes and fresh chocolate-filled cronuts, the croissant-donut combinations that were Bernice's specialty. I told him about Leif, Melissa and Ava.

"What's your take on it, Bernie? Should I really be supporting their decisions? Or should I voice objections? When it comes to Leif, I'm always of two minds and neither of them really clear-cut."

"Whatever you do, whatever you say, remember you don't want to sever your ties to Leif. Estranged families are so sad for all parties involved. Just keep those lines of communication open."

"Good advice, as usual. Thanks. It helps to share this with a friend whom I can trust to be wise and understanding."

Just as Bernie was preparing to leave, my phone rang. It was Marta in a panic about her mother, who suddenly was feeling strange. She said Christine's face was swelling, and she was dizzy and had a blazing headache and blurred vision. They were on their way to Doc. Schultz's office and I told her I would meet them there. My quiet, peace-filled day took a radical shift.

Bernie and I rushed to the parking lot only to find my old Honda and his new, sleek, black Chrysler covered with fluffy, dry snow. We brushed off our cars and Bernie wished me luck, then made the sign of the cross and said, "The Lord be with you."

I automatically replied, "And also with you," as I jumped into my car and sped to the doctor's office, which was located just off Main Street in the lower level of the old Victorian house where Doc Schultz and his wife Marion lived.

Marta and Christine were already in the living room which had been converted into an exam room, Christine on the exam table and Marta holding her hand. My wife gave me a weak smile, and I took her other hand as we listened to the doctor on the phone.

He finished his call and turned to me. "Hi Pastor. Christine's blood pressure is elevated and she is possibly having preeclampsia. The baby seems to be in a little distress, so she's off to the hospital. I think Methodist in Des Moines is the best place, especially since it's connected to Blank Children's where there is an outstanding NICU."

"NICU?"

"Neonatal Intensive Care Unit. In case the baby should need it."

I felt like my own blood pressure was rising. I was suddenly afraid for both my wife and our baby. "Marta and I will drive her down immediately."

The doctor shook his head. "Not fast enough. I've just talked with the police chief. He's sending over a cruiser to take Christine to the south parking lot of the wind power company outside of town. Methodist is sending a medevac helicopter to transport her. You and Marta can see her off and then head down to Des Moines."

"Can we go in the helicopter with her?"

"Some crews will allow a family member to go along, but some won't. It's probably best if you plan on driving, and then you'll have a car to get home."

I heard the squad car's siren growing louder as it came down the street. I bent down and whispered to my wife, "Hang on, sweetheart. I love you. Everything is going to be just fine. They'll take good care of you, and Marta and I will be there as soon as we can."

I could see that she was trying to be brave, but tears were leaking out of the corner of her eyes, and all she could seem to do was nod.

Everything proceeded in a whirlwind of activity and soon Christine was airborne and Marta and I were on the road. That's when the dancing snowflakes of earlier in the day turned into a heavy snowfall driven by howling winds. We crept down the interstate in near white-out conditions with the Honda's windshield wipers fighting to keep up with the ice forming on the blades. I spun out and managed to right the car after skirting the ditch, as Marta yelled, "Dad, Dad watch out. Slow down." The drive to Des Moines, which normally was about forty minutes, took us almost two hours.

We found Christine in the Family Birthing Center in a room that looked like a hotel room, nothing like the Maternity Ward of my memory. She was being attended to by a tiny woman with deep-set dark eyes and a sing-song accent.

"I am Dr. Chatterjee, a resident OB," she said extending her hand. "You are Mr. Henderson, I presume?"

Being called mister instead of pastor or reverend always threw me. Not wanting to explain, I merely answered, "Yes, and this is our daughter Marta."

"Mrs. Henderson and I were just discussing her options. Her preeclampsia is mild and we have her blood pressure stabilized. The fetal monitor shows the baby is doing fine. Nevertheless, I think that it is time for him to be born. He seems quite large, maybe over nine pounds already at 37 weeks. This is not uncommon with older mothers."

I went to the bed and took Christine's hand and kissed her forehead, as Dr. Chatterjee continued. "It is Christine's choice to start with induced labor, but I warned her that if it does not go quickly, we must take the baby by C-section. We artificially broke her membrane and administered Pitocin about five minutes ago. So we will see. Do you have any questions?"

"How long before we have to take the C-section option?" I asked.

"That all depends on how labor is progressing. I want to assure you that for high risk pregnancies such as this, we will be constantly monitoring your wife and the baby."

The words "high risk pregnancy" totally freaked me out. Feeling weak in the knees, I sat in the recliner next to Christine's bed.

She seemed remarkably calm. "Darling, I bet you and Marta haven't had any lunch. Go to the cafeteria and eat something. I promise not to have this baby before you return. And Marta, text your brother and tell him not to come until the weather has improved. I just saw an alert on the TV."

I looked up as she pointed to the television mounted high on the wall. The sound was muted, but the weather map was enough to show that we were in for a wicked storm.

Marta and I ate lukewarm tomato soup and greasy grilled cheese sandwiches in the hospital café. Marta pulled out her phone to text Leif.

"Oh, I think I forgot to lock the church. If he still has a key, ask him to go lock the door, please." My mind was racing trying to re-order my priorities, cover all the bases. How nice it would have been to have an associate pastor. "Do you think Leif can assemble a crib? I was meaning to do it after Christmas and…"

"Dad, calm down," Marta said as she put her arm around me. "You're acting a little loony. Dr. Chatterjee seems to be very competent and she said that a neonatal pediatrician named Dr. Mohammed was coming over from Children's. Mom's in capable medical hands and in God's hands, too."

A wonderfully crazy thought popped into my mind, the possibility that my wife was being attended by a Hindu and our newborn son by a Muslim. That would be good sermon fodder.

I only have snapshot images of what happened when we returned to the Birthing Center. Monitors were beeping and Dr. Chatterjee was calming giving orders. I remember putting on a surgical gown, mask and hat and going into the OR with Christine. I can see the scalpel making the incision that Christine later would refer to as her "permanent smile."

The next thing I remember is coming to on a couch in the lounge with Marta half crying and half laughing beside me. "I can't believe you passed out and missed it all, Dad."

A short, thin man in surgical garb, including a mask covering his beard, came out of the OR carrying our son. "You have a big boy, Mr. Henderson. I checked him over thoroughly and he is fine, 9 pounds 12 ounces and 21 inches long. Your wife is doing fine, too. When Dr. Chatterjee is finished suturing, she will come and talk with you."

He put the swaddled baby into my arms and I pulled aside the blanket to get my first look at his fat red face, puffy eyes and hairless head.

"Wow, he's beautiful, isn't he, Dad?" said Marta. "Or he will be when he loses some baby fat and grows some hair." We both got the giggles.

Chapter Eleven

Last Sunday in Advent/Christmas Eve

Hymn ##271 "I Am So Glad Each Christmas Eve"

With the last Sunday of Advent and Christmas Eve falling on the same day, this was a very busy day at First Lutheran. It had been a long time since I was not presiding over morning worship. Sarah, bless her heart, had arranged for the associate pastor from Bethesda Lutheran in Ames to fill in for me for the morning service. I planned to be back in Turners Bend for the 7:00 p.m. Candlelight Christmas Eve service, along with Christine and our new son.

Seasoned solo pastors sometimes think that a congregation can't function without them, but reports from Sarah indicated they were doing fine. The poinsettias were delivered, as well as fresh hay for the stable. Supplies of wine, bread and candles were checked. My robe was laundered and pressed. All would be ready when I returned. It was a good lesson in humility for me. I wasn't indispensable after all.

Our stay in the Family Birthing Center had been extended. Leif drove down to see us and to take Marta home. I remained cocooned with Christine and the baby in our luxury suite. We weathered a couple of setbacks. The baby's bilirubin count rose sharply and his skin and eyes turned yellow. Fortunately the blue-green spectrum lights he was put under reduced the jaundice and returned him to a rosy color. Christine got a bladder infection and was pretty miserable for a couple days.

We bonded with the baby, sleeping when he slept and awaking with him at odd hours. The room was equipped with a laptop and Wi-Fi. I was able to communicate with the outside world, send emails and photos and view the Facebook page that Marta put up for us.

I related an email message from Marta to Christine as she nursed the baby. "Marta says that the refrigerator and freezer are so full of food from our friends that we won't have to shop until the snow melts. Bernice is helping her prepare our Christmas Eve dinner.

"And here's another email from her. It seems that Lance Williams helped Leif assemble the crib and Lucinda swept in and decorated the nursery in a Teddy Bear motif."

"Oh dear. With being on bed rest, I didn't get a chance to finish the nursery, but I sure hope Lucinda didn't go over the top on glitz and kitsch."

"I'm sure it will be an eye-popper, but tasteful. Marta says that your women's group just delivered diapers, wipes, and lots of other essentials, so the room will be move-in ready. She also says that everyone is asking about the baby's name."

"Mark, I don't want to leave here with a birth certificate that just says Baby Boy. We have to decide on his name," she said.

"I've been thinking a lot about biblical couples who were surprised to become parents at an old age, what about the names of their sons?"

"Are you thinking of Sarah and Abraham's son for the first name and Elizabeth and Zechariah's son for the second?"

"Yes, what do you say?"

She paused and switched the baby from one breast to the other. "I like it, but I still want to use my great grandfather's name, too."

"How about Gunnar as a third name?" I said as a concession.

Christine laughed. "That will be quite a moniker, but I love it."

***

Getting discharged from the hospital took longer than I had expected, and the three of us arrived at First Lutheran just an hour before the Christmas Eve service was to begin. The parking lot was a veritable zoo.

In the past our nativity scene had been furnished with large molded-plastic figures and animals. But, apparently that would not do for our new, architecturally-designed stable. All the men who had constructed the stable were dressed as shepherds. There were sheep and goats running around the yard, baaing and bleating. A Shetland pony was tethered to a post. Dr. Jane was trying unsuccessfully to unload a Holstein from a trailer, but the cow seemed to have something else in mind entirely. And there were dogs, lots of large breed pets and farm dogs

59

with thick coats, including a Great Dane that was bigger than the pony.

Spotlights were directed onto the scene and a twinkling star-light beamed above the stable, suspended by a wire. People were ankle-deep in snow and several animals were doing their business wherever they pleased.

Inside the stable were Leif, garbed as Joseph, and Melissa as Mary. I assumed the screaming baby, swaddled and lying in the manger was a very unhappy Ava.

Rather than a holy, serene scene, it was chaotic and wonderful at the same time. People were snapping cellphone pictures and laughing, and children were running after animals. It was wild and wooly and full of joy.

I began to worry that I would never get everyone to come inside to worship, much less with the reverence that the day called for, but eventually they did and our traditional choir procession of "O Come All Ye Faithful" began up the aisle. I followed them and stood before the altar, facing the congregation.

"We begin in the name of the Father, the Son and the Holy Spirit," I said, as I glanced over to the front pew on the pulpit side. Last Fall Christine sat alone in that pew. Now the whole pew was full of my family, our sons, our daughter and our possibly-future daughter-in-law and granddaughter. My cup of blessing was over-flowing, as we clergy like to say.

I recited the passages in Luke that I long ago memorized and preached my Prince of Peace sermon.

"Many of you have heard this sermon before. In fact, it is the same sermon I have preached every Christmas Eve that I have been your pastor here at First Lutheran, nineteen years. It's not because I can't come up with another message; it's that there really is only one message for this most holy of days. God sent us the Prince of Peace in the form of an infant child. The child who even today works for peace, peace in the world, peace in our country, peace in our town, peace in our families, and most of all, peace in our hearts. It is the peace that passes all understanding."

When I concluded the rest of my message, I asked all the children to come forth and stand around the baptismal font. They poured out of the pews, little girls in sparkly dressed and patent leather shoes, little boys in vests and bow ties or sweaters knit for them by their grandmothers, tween girls in long black velvet outfits, hobbling on their first pair of high-heeled shoes, tween boys in stiff new button-down shirts. Some came hesitantly and others boldly, the precious children of our congregation.

I called forth Christine, with our baby boy in her arms, and Leif and Marta as his sponsors, and I christened our son. "Isaac John Gunnar Henderson, child of God, you have been sealed by the Holy Spirit and marked with the cross of Christ forever."

I took Isaac in my arms and held him up to introduce him to our members. He seemed to smile and then spit up sour milk all over the sleeve of my robe.

"Eew," said Junior James in his newly-developed stage voice. "The kid just puked all over Pastor Mark." There was laughing and clapping and the flashing of a few cameras. This would be a story that Isaac would probably hear for the rest of his life, I thought.

The service ended, as we always concluded, with the singing of "Silent Night" and the passing of lighted candles in the dimly-light sanctuary. And peace came down to us at First Lutheran Church in Turners Bend, Iowa.

Chapter Twelve

Christmas Morning

Hymn # "Infant Holy, Infant Lowly"

In the predawn morning I rocked Isaac in the antique rocking chair that Lois and Hjalmer Gustafson had gifted us. The arms and seat of the oak chair were grooved and worn smooth by the many parents who soothed their infants in it for decades, perhaps humming or singing as I was. I sang through all my favorite Christmas carols and was surprised at the number of verses I had committed to memory.

"Daddy will soon have to get dressed in his clerical collar and go to church for the Christmas Day service of lessons and carols, but Mommy and your brother and sister will be here to watch over you. Then I will come home, change into sweats and show you how to make Swedish pancakes. We will open gifts and play games and watch movies and snack on goodies all day. Okay?"

He looked at me with wide eyes, as if I was preaching the gospel. I sang "Rock-a-bye Baby" and he drifted off to sleep. I put my nose to his head and inhaled his wondrous sweet-baby smell.

Just one month ago I was despairing of the coming season and another Advent and Christmas at First Lutheran. I had conflicted feelings about becoming a parent again and about how a baby would change my life plans. I was in an oh-woe-is-me mood. I was tired of carrying the load of my ministry alone or what I thought at the time was alone.

Simply said, God showed me the error of my ways. I whispered a prayer of thanksgiving and praise.

Amen.

Author Notes

If you enjoyed this journey to Turners Bend, Iowa, please check out the Can Be Murder series by Marilyn Rausch and Mary Donlon. Visit our website at:

www.rauschanddonlonauthors.com

Or view the Rausch and Donlon Facebook page.

Headaches Can Be Murder and *Love Can Be Murder* are available in paperback and eBook versions. Coming soon: *Writing Can Be Murder.*

If you want to read more about Bernice, the waitress at the Cinnamon Bun Café, download *Sweet Dreams: Recipes From a Lifetime in Turners Bend.*

Made in the USA
Charleston, SC
19 August 2014